Flamingos

Quinn M. Arnold

CREATIVE EDUCATION • CREATIVE PAPERBACKS

seedlings

Published by Creative Education and Creative Paperbacks
P.O. Box 227, Mankato, Minnesota 56002
Creative Education and Creative Paperbacks
are imprints of The Creative Company
www.thecreativecompany.us

Design by Ellen Huber; production by Joe Kahnke
Art direction by Rita Marshall
Printed in China

Photographs by Alamy (epa european pressphoto agency b.v.),
Getty Images (Nikki O'Keefe Images), iStockphoto (jamcgraw,
Roberto_Marcon, mjf99), Minden Pictures (Bill Coster, Elliott
Neep), National Geographic Creative (JOEL SARTORE/NATIONAL
GEOGRAPHIC PHOTO ARK), Shutterstock (cyo bo, Sebastien
Burel, Le Do, Svetlana Foote, Christian Musat, Anna Om,
Roby1960, Auttapol Sangsub, topseller, worldswildlifewonders),
SuperStock (Roger Eritja/age fotostock, NHPA/NHPA)

Library of Congress Cataloging-in-Publication Data
Names: Arnold, Quinn M., author.
Title: Flamingos / Quinn M. Arnold.
Series: Seedlings.
Includes index.
Summary: A kindergarten-level introduction to flamingos,
covering their growth process, behaviors, the lakes they call
home, and such defining features as their long legs.
Identifiers: LCCN 2016054472 / ISBN 978-1-60818-867-3
(hardcover) / ISBN 978-1-62832-482-2 (pbk) / ISBN 978-1-
56660-915-9 (eBook)

Subjects: LCSH: Flamingos—Juvenile literature.
Classification: LCC QL696.C56 A78 2017 / DDC 598.3/5—dc23

CCSS: RI.K.1, 2, 3, 4, 5, 6, 7;
RI.1.1, 2, 3, 4, 5, 6, 7; RF.K.1, 3; RF.1.1

First Edition HC 9 8 7 6 5 4 3 2 1
First Edition PBK 9 8 7 6 5 4 3 2 1

TABLE OF CONTENTS

Hello,
flamingos!

Flamingos are tall birds. They live by warm, salty water.

They form big flocks.

Most flamingos are pink. They can be orange or red, too. Flamingo wings have black feathers.

Flamingos have long necks. Their **bills** are bent.

They stand
on one thin
leg to rest.

A flamingo turns its head upside down to eat.

It swings its bill back and forth. It catches shrimp. It eats algae, too.

A chick is a baby flamingo.
It comes out of an egg.

The chick is gray and fluffy. Its parents take care of it.

Flamingos run
across water.

They flap their wings
and fly into the air.

Goodbye, flamingos!

Picture a Flamingo

feathers

neck

legs

wings

eye

ankle

bill

foot

Words to Know

algae: groups of plants that do not have leaves or stems and grow in water

bills: beaks, or parts of birds' faces that stick out

feathers: parts of a bird's body that grow out of its skin

flocks: large groups of birds that live together

Read More

Gibbs, Maddie. *Flamingos.*
New York: PowerKids Press, 2011.

Riggs, Kate. *Flamingos.*
Mankato, Minn.: Creative Education, 2015.

Websites

All Things Animal TV: Flamingos
https://www.youtube.com/watch?v=Pz3XiJac57w
Watch a video to learn more about flamingos.

Super Coloring: Flamingos Coloring Pages
http://www.supercoloring.com/coloring-pages
/birds/flamingos
Print off pictures of flamingos to color.

Index